Paperback ISBN 979-8-9865811-9-4
Hardcover ISBN 979-8-9865811-8-7
Ebook ISBN 979-8-9865811-7-0

FOR CHANDLER, CHLOE, LYLA, BENTLEY, AND BRODY. I LOVE YOU ALL VERY MUCH, AND YOUR DADS' MEMORIES WILL LIVE ON FOREVER.

SHE TELLS ME YOU'RE A SPIRIT WHO
WILL ALWAYS BE WITH ME.
I NEED YOU HERE IN PERSON NOW.
IT'S WHAT I WANT TO SEE.

7

WE'D BE RIDING DIRTBIKES QUICKLY ON THE TRAILS AND THROUGH THE MUD,

I ALWAYS WAKE HOPING YOU'LL
BE STANDING BY MY BED.

"MY DADDY'S COMING HOME TODAY!"
I'VE SAID, AND SAID, AND SAID.

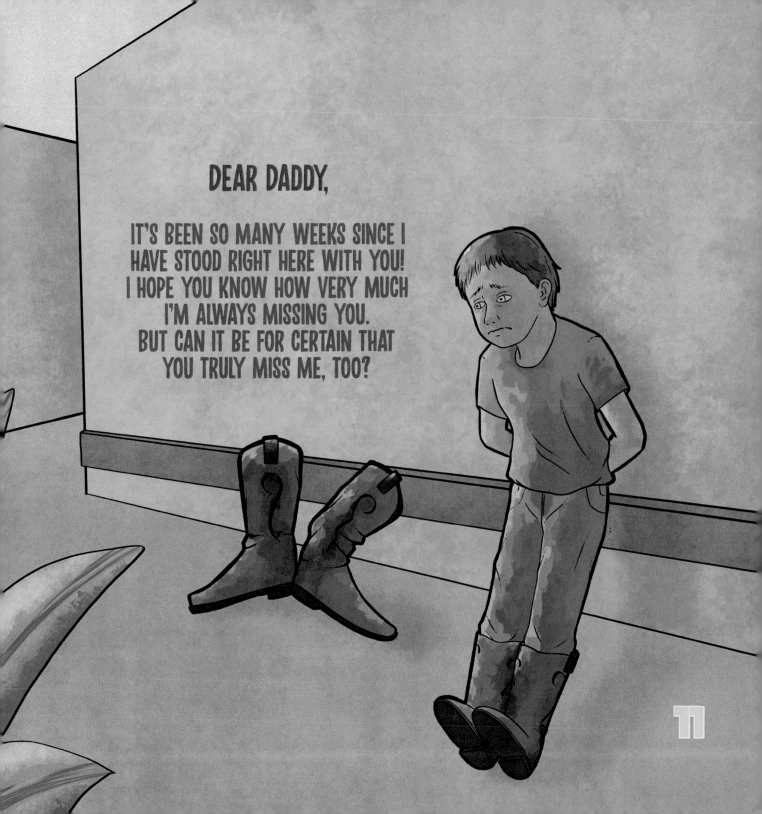

I HATE MY MOM BECAUSE OF WHAT
SHE'S ALWAYS TELLING ME.
I HATE YOU, DADDY, TOO!
WHY DID YOU GO AWAY FROM ME?

DEAR DADDY,
OH DADDY,
IF YOU DO COME BACK,
I'LL PICK UP ALL MY TOYS.

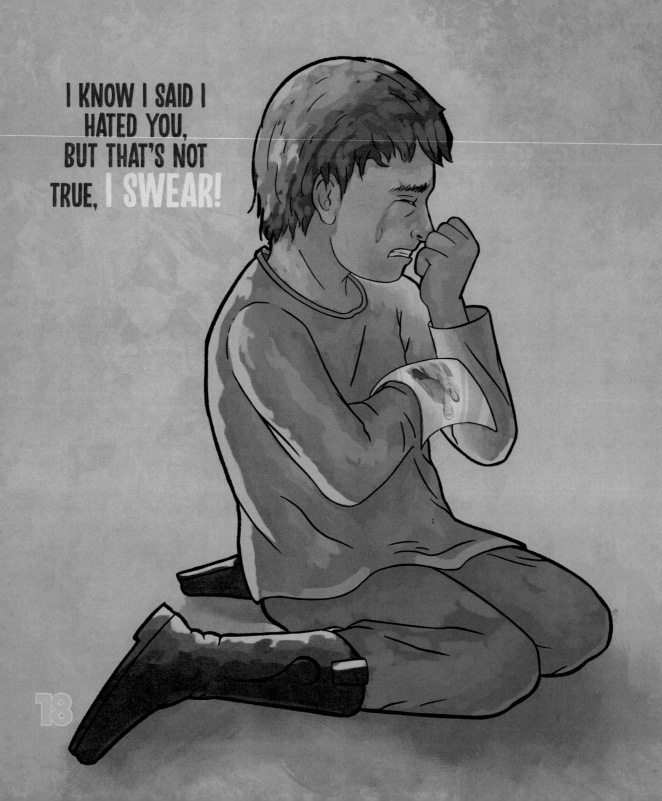

PLEASE COME BACK NOW,
AND SHOW ME THAT
YOU REALLY, TRULY CARE!

I PROMISE TO BE GOOD AND DO
JUST ANYTHING FOR YOU,
CAUSE HAVING YOU AT HOME WOULD BE
MY GREATEST DREAM COME TRUE!

DEAR DADDY,
I HAVEN'T SEEN YOU IN A WHILE
I MISS YOUR LAUGH, YOUR VOICE,
YOUR SMILE.
SO ALL I DO THESE DAYS IS CRY
I SIMPLY CAN'T IMAGINE WHY.
I'M SCARED OF LOSING MOMMY, TOO.
AND WHEN SHE'S GONE,
IT MAKES ME BLUE.

20

WHEN YOU'RE NOT HERE,
IT'S JUST NO FUN.
I DO NOT WANT
TO SEE THE SUN.
SO PLEASE DON'T MAKE
ME RIDE MY BIKE,

AND PLEASE DON'T
MAKE ME GO AND HIKE.
I DO NOT WANT TO GO
AND SLIDE.
I REALLY WANT TO RUN
AND HIDE.

21

DEAR DADDY,
I'VE NOTICED SINCE
THE TIME YOU LEFT,
IT'S BEEN SO VERY STRANGE!

22

THOUGH MEMORIES
CAN MAKE ME WEEP,
THEY'RE TREASURES THAT
I'LL ALWAYS KEEP.

27